The Dance Fairies

For my cousin Becky,

who could outwit the goblins every time,

Special thanks to

Narinder Dhami

ORCHARD BOOKS
338 Euston Road, London NW1 3BH
Orchard Books Australia
Level 17/207 Kent Street, Sydney, NSW 2000
A Paperback Original

First published in 2007 by Orchard Books

A CIP catalogue record for this book is available
from the British Library.

ISBN 978 1 84616 490 3
1 3 5 7 9 10 8 6 4 2

Printed in Great Britain

Orchard Books is a division of Hachette Children's Books,
an Hachette Livre cUK company

www.orchardbooks.co.uk

Bethany the Ballet Fairy

by Daisy Meadows

www.rainbowmagic.co.uk

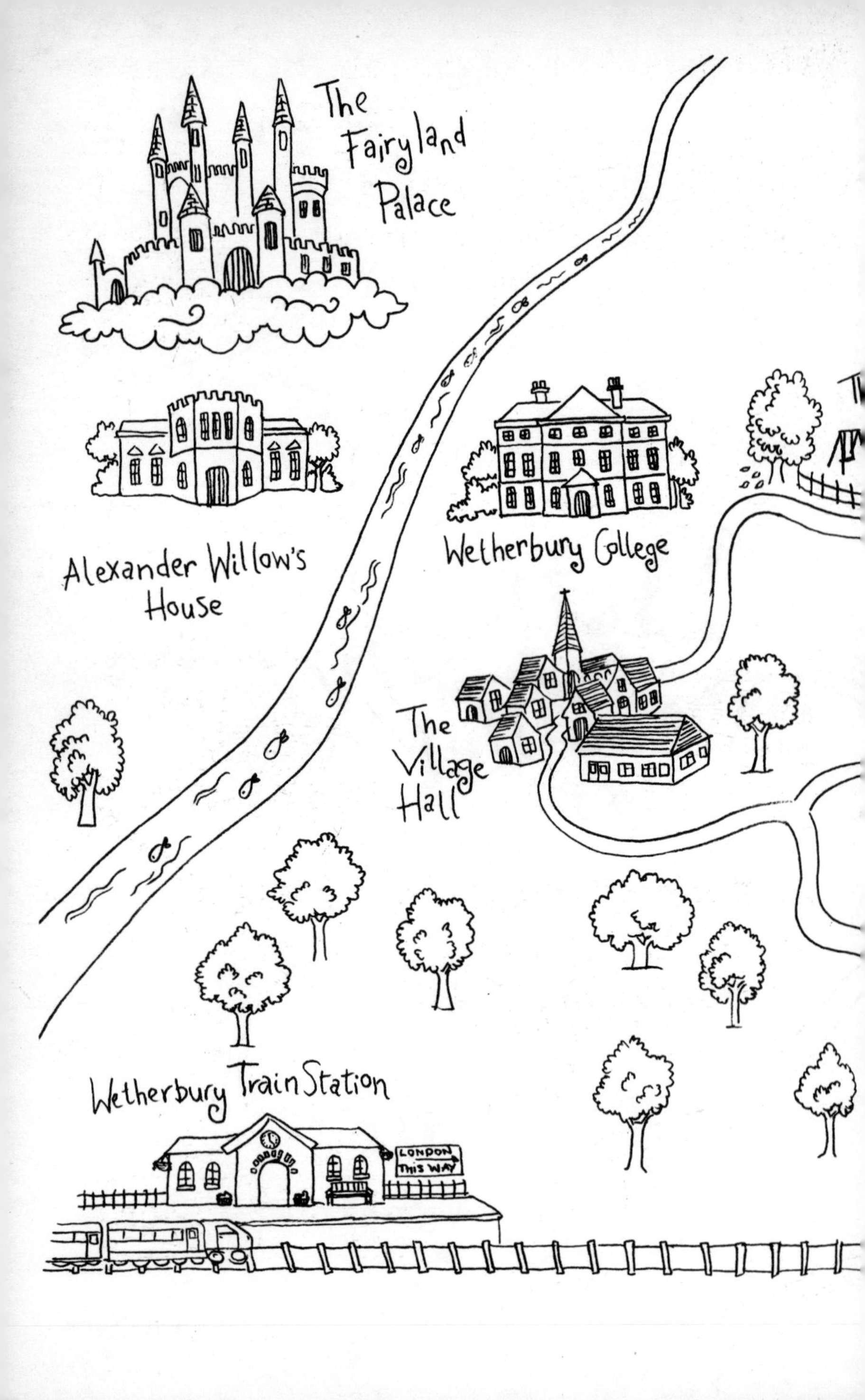
The Fairyland Palace
Alexander Willow's House
Wetherbury College
The Village Hall
Wetherbury Train Station
LONDON THIS WAY

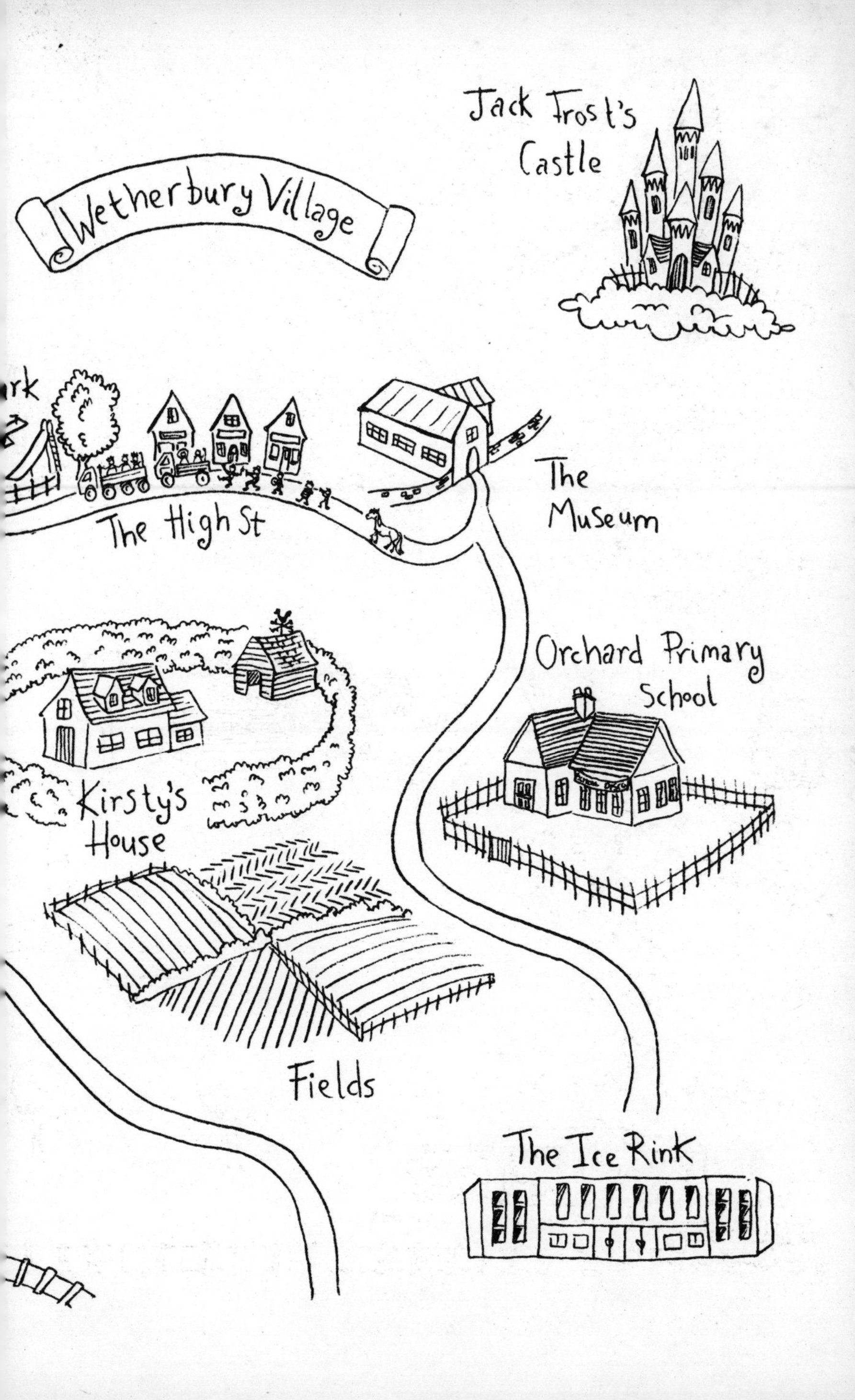
Jack Frost's
Castle
Wetherbury Village
The High St
The
Museum
Orchard Primary
School
Kirsty's
House
Fields
The Ice Rink

Hold tight to the ribbons, please.
You goblins now may feel a breeze.
I'm summoning a hurricane
To take the ribbons away again.

But, goblins, you'll be swept up too,
For I have work for you to do.
Guard each ribbon carefully,
By using this new power to freeze.

Contents

"I'm *really* looking forward to this!" exclaimed Rachel Walker to her best friend, Kirsty Tate. "I *love* ballet."

"Me, too," Kirsty agreed, raising her voice above the noise of the train as it rattled over a bumpy bit of track. "I've never seen *Swan Lake* before."

"I've heard that this is a fantastic

production," Kirsty's mum said. "The scenery is supposed to be gorgeous."

"Well, let's hope it keeps Dad awake!" Kirsty laughed, glancing at her dad who was fast asleep in the corner seat. "I'm so pleased you could come, Rachel. Wasn't it lucky that your school finished for half-term the day before ours? You wouldn't have been here in time to come with us otherwise."

Rachel nodded. Because their families lived quite a long way apart, she was staying with Kirsty for the whole week of the half-term holiday.

"We'll be in London soon," said

Mrs Tate, as the train drew into a station. "This is the last stop before we get there."

Kirsty stared out of the window as the train slowed. Suddenly her attention was caught by a flash of icy blue streaking past the window. Puzzled, Kirsty leaned forward for a closer look.

To her amazement, she saw seven little fairies being tumbled through the air by a tiny icy whirlwind. As Kirsty watched, the fairies landed safely in one of the baskets of flowers suspended from the station roof.

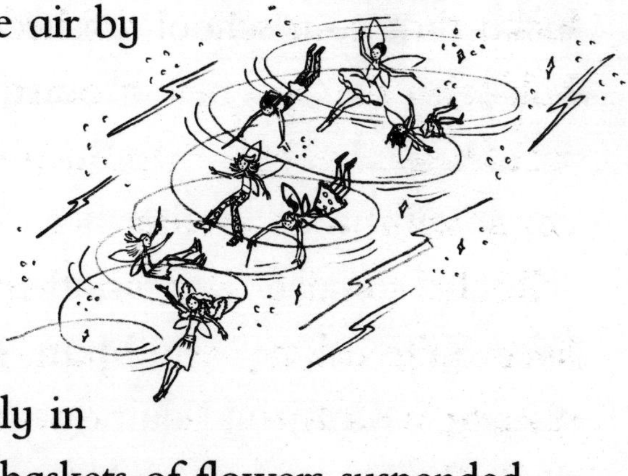

Kirsty and Rachel knew a lot about fairies because the two girls shared an amazing secret. They were best friends with the fairies, and had often helped them to defeat mean Jack Frost and his naughty goblin servants, who were always causing trouble. Now it looked as if their fairy friends might need the girls' help once more.

Almost bursting with excitement, Kirsty glanced at Rachel. But she could see that her friend hadn't noticed anything.

"Mum, I'm feeling hungry," Kirsty said quickly. "Do you think Rachel and I could go and get some biscuits from the buffet car?"

Mrs Tate nodded. "But not too many," she warned. "Remember we're going out for dinner after the show."

Kirsty nodded as she and Rachel got up from their seats.

"Rachel, I've just seen *seven* fairies on the station platform!" Kirsty gasped, as soon as they'd left the carriage.

Rachel looked thrilled. "Seven fairies!" she exclaimed. "Where?"

"Right here!" Kirsty said, pulling down the window that lay directly opposite the basket of fairies. "Hello!" she called softly, hoping the fairies would hear her.

The fairies were dusting themselves off among the pansies, but at the sound of Kirsty's voice, one of them looked up and saw the girls. Her tiny face lit up, and a moment later all seven fairies were zooming over to join Kirsty and Rachel. They flew inside the train and Kirsty shut the window.

"You're Rachel and Kirsty!" declared one of the fairies, happily. "I've seen you with the King and Queen in Fairyland."

The girls smiled at the tiny fairy, who was dressed in a sparkling white tutu and pink ballet shoes. "I'm so pleased you're here," the fairy went on. "We're the Dance Fairies. I'm Bethany the Ballet Fairy, and this is Jade the Disco Fairy, Rebecca the Rock 'n' Roll Fairy, Tasha the Tap Dance Fairy, Jessica the Jazz Fairy, Saskia the Salsa Fairy and Imogen the Ice Dance Fairy."

Rachel and Kirsty smiled at the fairies, feeling quite dazzled by their gorgeous outfits. The fairies managed to smile back, but the girls could see that their eyes were sad and their sparkling wings drooped.

"Has something gone wrong?" asked Rachel.

Bethany nodded. "It's Jack Frost!" she announced miserably. "He's just cast a spell to throw us out of Fairyland and into the human world. That's why we're here. But, worst of all, he's stolen our magic Dance Ribbons!"

Jack Frost Spells Trouble

"Oh, no!" Rachel exclaimed. "Jack Frost's up to his old tricks again!"

"What exactly do the ribbons do?" asked Kirsty.

"They make sure that all dancing goes well and is fun, both in Fairyland and in the human world," Bethany explained. "But the ribbons will only work properly if they are each attached to the right fairy's wand. If we don't get our ribbons back, nobody will be able to dance properly ever again!"

Rachel and Kirsty stared at each other in horror.

"That's terrible!" Kirsty exclaimed.

"Is there anything we can do to help?" Rachel asked.

Bethany smiled gratefully at them. "Thank you, girls!" she cried. "Even though Jack Frost's spell cast us into the human world, a little bit of fairy magic must have helped to bring us here to you! Will you come to Fairyland with us, so that we can tell the King and

Queen what's happened?"

"We'd love to, but what about my mum and dad?" asked Kirsty. "They'll wonder where we are."

"Fairy magic will make sure you return to the human world as if no time has passed," Bethany replied reassuringly.

Rachel and Kirsty grinned and Bethany showered the girls with white and pink glittering fairy dust. As the magical sparkles floated down around them, the girls shrank to fairy-size and translucent wings appeared on their shoulders.

Next moment, the girls were whizzing through the air in a haze of fairy dust, and, in no time at all, they were hovering above the golden Fairyland palace with its four pink turrets.

The King and Queen were strolling in the palace gardens. They looked extremely surprised to see the seven Dance Fairies, as well as Rachel and Kirsty, fluttering towards them.

"Good afternoon, Dance Fairies!"

King Oberon called. "And welcome, Kirsty and Rachel."

"How are you, girls?" asked Queen Titania, smiling kindly at Kirsty and Rachel. "Do you need our help?"

"No, Your Majesty," Rachel replied, shaking her head.

"It's us Dance Fairies who need Kirsty and Rachel's help, Your Majesties!" Bethany declared. "Jack Frost has just stolen our magic Dance Ribbons!"

The King and Queen frowned.

"He sent us all hurtling into the human world too," Bethany went on. "But, luckily, fairy magic led us to Kirsty and Rachel, and then we all came back to Fairyland to tell you what had happened."

"Let's see exactly what went on," said Queen Titania, leading the way to the golden pool in the palace gardens. The Queen waved her wand over the pool and then nodded at Bethany.

The Ballet Fairy immediately touched her wand gently to the water and ripples began to spread across its surface.

"As Your Majesties already know, Jack Frost was fed up because whenever he throws a party, none of his goblins can dance properly!" Bethany explained. "So today, Jack Frost asked the other Dance Fairies and me to teach the goblins how to dance."

"We thought it meant that Jack Frost had changed his ways and wanted to be friends with us," Jade the Disco Fairy put in. "But we were wrong!"

Everyone watched as a picture appeared in the pool. Rachel and Kirsty saw the seven Dance Fairies knocking on the door of Jack Frost's ice castle.

"Are those the magic ribbons?" asked Kirsty, pointing at the fairies' wands in the picture. Each fairy had a ribbon trailing from the tip of her wand.

Bethany nodded as the picture changed to show Jack Frost opening the door. His cold, sulky face broke into a smile as he saw the Dance Fairies waiting outside.

"Come in!" he cried, "We're all ready for you!"

Rachel and Kirsty watched as Jack Frost led the Dance Fairies into the throne room. There his goblin servants were lined up, dressed in their finest outfits. They wore outsized hats with large plumed feathers, embroidered waistcoats and velvet trousers. Rachel and Kirsty smiled. They'd never seen the goblins look quite like this before!

Jack Frost sat down on his magnificent ice throne, and watched as the Dance Fairies began the lesson.

The goblins were *terrible* dancers.

They stumbled across the throne room, frequently tripping over their own feet and each other's. Then they started arguing, and their yelling drowned out the beautiful music that the Dance Fairies had conjured up.

But, as Rachel and Kirsty watched, the Dance Fairies quickly began to work their magic. Gradually the goblins stopped bumping into each other and arguing, and began gliding around the room in time to the music instead.

Kirsty nudged Rachel. "Look, even Jack Frost seems to be enjoying himself!" she pointed out.

Jack Frost was sitting on his throne, merrily tapping his foot along to the music. But, suddenly, he jumped up from his seat, a spiteful smile on his face.

"NOW!" he bellowed.

Immediately the goblins dashed forward and grabbed all seven ribbons from the Dance Fairies' wands. Whooping with glee, they then began waving the ribbons triumphantly in the air.

The fairies were taken completely by surprise, but they quickly raised their wands to cast a spell.

Unfortunately, they were too late. Jack Frost was already pointing his wand at them, and shouting a spell of his own. "Come, freezing wind and ice and snow. To the human world, Dance Fairies, GO!"

Instantly, an icy wind whistled through the throne room. Rachel and Kirsty watched in horror as the Dance Fairies were swept up in the freezing whirlwind and carried out of the window.

"So *that's* how we ended up in the human world!" Bethany sighed, as the images in the pool faded. "And that's how Jack Frost got our ribbons!"

Ribbons Whisked Away

"We *must* get the ribbons back," King Oberon declared.

"We'll all go to Jack Frost's ice castle immediately!" Queen Titania decided.

She waved her wand and Kirsty and Rachel heard a bell tinkling in the distance. A few moments later there was the sound of hooves, and a carriage

made of shining crystal drew up outside the palace gates. The carriage was drawn by six unicorns with gleaming white coats and crystal horns. They came to a halt, tossing their snowy manes and neighing softly.

"Look, it's Bertram!" Rachel pointed out as the King and Queen led them over to the carriage.

Bertram, the frog footman, was sitting at the front of the carriage. He gave the girls a cheery wave.

Kirsty and Rachel climbed in and sat down next to the King and Queen on pink velvet cushions. Meanwhile the Dance Fairies perched on the unicorns' backs, and the carriage set off through Fairyland.

It wasn't long before they'd left the beautiful green meadows behind. Rachel and Kirsty shivered as the temperature began to fall.

"There's Jack Frost's ice castle," Rachel said. The girls had visited the castle before, but it was still very scary-looking. It stood on a tall hill under a gloomy sky, and it was built of sheets of ice with towers topped by icy blue turrets.

"And there's Jack Frost!" Kirsty added, as a head poked out of one of the windows.

Jack Frost scowled when he saw the carriage approaching, and ducked back inside the castle again.

"Somehow, I don't think he wants to return the magic ribbons!" Rachel remarked.

The carriage drew up beside the castle and Bertram hopped down to help everyone out. But, as they made their way towards the heavy castle door, it was suddenly flung open and Jack Frost stalked out.

"You're too late!" he snapped. "The ribbons are gone, and there's nothing you can do about it!"

A great shriek above their heads made

Rachel, Kirsty and all the fairies glance upwards. They saw a goblin fly out of one of the castle windows, carried along by a huge whirlwind. He was clutching a pink ribbon which flapped in the breeze.

"That's my magic ribbon!" Bethany cried. She tried to fly towards the shrieking goblin, but the icy whirlwind pushed her back. In fact, the wind was so strong that Rachel, Kirsty and the others could hardly keep their feet on the ground.

"There's more of them!" Rachel shouted, pointing upwards.

Six more goblins were tumbling through the air. Each of them holding on to a different ribbon.

"I command you to return the magic ribbons, Jack Frost!" King Oberon cried. Battling against the wind, the King lifted his wand and murmured some magic words. Immediately, the wind dropped, but the goblins had already vanished. Rachel and Kirsty glanced at each other in dismay.

"You're coming with us, Jack Frost!" King Oberon said sternly. "And you'll stay under guard at our palace until all the ribbons are returned to the Dance Fairies."

"Oh, but you'll *never* get the ribbons back!" Jack Frost cackled. "I've told my goblin servants to hide in the human world, and there they'll stay! And besides..." he added, pausing and looking even more sly than usual. "Even if the fairies *do* find my goblins, they'll soon see that this time there's more to them than meets the eye!"

And he laughed even louder.

King Oberon sighed and waved his wand again. A swirl of fairy dust lifted Jack Frost off his feet and swept him into the royal carriage.

The doors slammed shut and Jack Frost's smile vanished.

"Girls, the goblins are hiding with the Dance Ribbons in the human world!" said Queen Titania, turning to Rachel and Kirsty. "Will you help the Dance Fairies to find them and get them back?

Rachel and Kirsty nodded solemnly.

"Each ribbon is attracted to its own type of dance," Bethany explained, "so each ribbon's magic will draw the goblin towards places where that ribbon's style of dance is taking place."

"Oh!" Rachel exclaimed. "We're going to the ballet tonight. Maybe the goblin with the Ballet Ribbon will be there!"

Bethany looked very excited. "I'll come with you, just in case!" she said.

Queen Titania was already lifting her wand to shower them with magic. "Good luck!" she called.

Looking more hopeful, the other Dance Fairies waved farewell, as Queen Titania's magic whisked Bethany, Rachel and Kirsty away. A moment later they were back on the train.

"We'd better go and buy some biscuits or Mum will wonder why we're back empty-handed!" Kirsty said, as Bethany hid in Rachel's pocket.

"We're almost there, girls," Mrs Tate said when Kirsty and Rachel arrived back from the buffet car. Mr Tate had woken up and they were gathering their things together.

Outside the station they took a cab to the ballet. As they went inside the theatre and took their seats, Rachel and Kirsty were amazed to see how beautiful it was. There were sweeping gold balconies, a domed roof painted with ballet scenes, and golden chairs with plush red cushions.

"Are you OK, Bethany?" Rachel whispered as the lights began to dim. Immediately the fairy peeped out of Rachel's pocket and smiled.

The curtain rose, and Kirsty and Rachel gasped as they gazed at the wintry scene before them. A huge frozen lake surrounded by leafless trees covered most of the stage, and a full moon hung in the sky. Everything was covered with frost which sparkled under the bright stage lights. Dancers in feathery white tutus were poised, motionless, here and there.

"It's lovely!" Rachel breathed, and Kirsty nodded.

They waited breathlessly for the ballet to begin, but none of the dancers moved a muscle. Puzzled, Rachel and Kirsty glanced at each other as the spectators began murmuring in confusion.

"Why is nobody dancing?" whispered Mrs Tate.

"This is all very strange!" Mr Tate added.

"Something's not right," Bethany whispered to Rachel and Kirsty. "And I'm sure it has something to do with Jack Frost's goblins!"

Still the dancers didn't move. The curtain fell, and the mutterings of the audience grew louder.

"We must try to save the ballet!" Bethany said urgently.

Rachel nodded. "We need to find that goblin!" she said.

"Dad, can we go and get

a programme?" Kirsty asked quickly.

Mr Tate nodded. "Don't be long though," he said. "I'm sure the ballet will start again soon."

"We should start backstage," Bethany told the girls as they hurried out into the lobby.

"But we'll need to make sure that we're not seen," Kirsty pointed out anxiously.

They ran to the back of the theatre and cautiously Rachel pushed open the stage door. A doorman sat in a little booth just inside the entrance.

"He's not moving," Kirsty whispered.

"And look!" Rachel added, as they went further backstage. "Neither is anyone else!"

All around them were stagehands who had been moving scenery, and dancers who had been warming up. But every single person was now completely frozen in place.

"They're as cold as ice!" Kirsty said, touching one of the dancer's arms. "Maybe Jack Frost has given his goblins a wand of ice magic."

"Listen!" said Bethany suddenly, "I can hear someone giggling!"

"It's coming from the other side of the stage," Rachel said.

Quickly the friends hurried across the curtained stage, weaving their way in and out of the motionless dancers. As they neared the other side, they saw a very strange sight.

A goblin wearing pink tights was struggling to get into a fluffy white tutu. He had jammed a pair of dainty white ballet shoes onto his feet, and around his head he had tied Bethany's pink Ballet Ribbon – larger now that it was in the

human world – in a neat bow.

Rachel and Kirsty put their hands over their mouths to muffle their giggles.

"I thought the goblins were supposed to be hiding," Kirsty whispered. "This one isn't doing a very good job of it!"

"The magic of the ribbons is so strong that anyone who has one can't help but dance!" Bethany explained, fluttering out of Rachel's pocket. "Come on, let's get my ribbon back!"

The goblin was so busy trying to squeeze into the tutu, he didn't notice Bethany and the girls until they were right in front of him. Kirsty was glad to see that he didn't seem to have a magic wand, either.

"Give my magic ribbon back, please!" Bethany said firmly.

The goblin scowled at her. "Go away, pesky fairy!" he muttered. "I'm not giving the ribbon back! I like being good at dancing. And, even better, I'm ruining the ballet for everyone else! Jack Frost is going to be *very* pleased with me."

"That's mean," Kirsty said.

The goblin looked thoughtful. Then suddenly he smiled sweetly at Kirsty. "Well, OK," he said. "You can take

the ribbon, but you'll have to untie it for me. I did it up too tightly."

Rachel frowned, feeling suspicious. Why was the goblin being so nice all of a sudden?

"Kirsty, don't—" Rachel began. But she was too late. Kirsty had already stepped forward to undo the ribbon. And as she did so, the goblin touched her wrist and said, "Freeze!"

Instantly, poor Kirsty was frozen stiff.

The goblin roared with laughter.

"Oh, no!" Rachel gasped, staring in horror at her frozen friend.

"Jack Frost must have given the goblins freezing powers," Bethany guessed. "So that's what he meant when he said there was more to the goblins than meets the eye!"

The goblin stepped forward, and reached out a big green hand towards Rachel.

"Oh, no, you don't!" Bethany cried, waving her wand over Rachel, and transforming her instantly into a tiny fairy. Rachel zoomed away from the goblin's touch and joined Bethany, out of his reach.

"Teehee!" the goblin chuckled. "You can't touch me, or I'll freeze you too!" And still laughing, he ran onto the stage.

"What are we going to do about Kirsty?" Rachel asked anxiously as she and Bethany flew after him.

"Don't worry, Rachel," Bethany said,

as they perched in one of the cardboard trees. "The spell will wear off soon and Kirsty will be fine."

Below them on the stage the goblin had begun to dance. Rachel's eyes widened as he performed perfect jetés, pirouettes and arabesques.

"He's a brilliant dancer!" she said.

"It's only because he's got my magic ribbon," Bethany sniffed. "We must get it back!"

Rachel watched the goblin moving around the stage and in and out of the wings. He was touching all the ballerinas and stagehands as he went past them, and Rachel guessed he was making sure they all remained frozen.

Suddenly Rachel noticed the large, pale moon, made out of tissue paper,

hanging from the top of the stage. It was suspended in the air from a rope, and as she looked at it, an idea popped into her head.

"Bethany," she whispered, "if the goblin was underneath the paper moon, we could drop it down on him and grab the ribbon!"

"Great idea, Rachel!" Bethany agreed eagerly. "It's very light, so it won't hurt him. But how will we get the goblin to stand underneath it?"

Rachel frowned. But before she could suggest anything, she saw Kirsty hurry

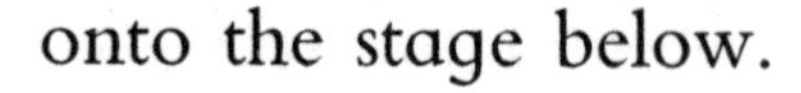

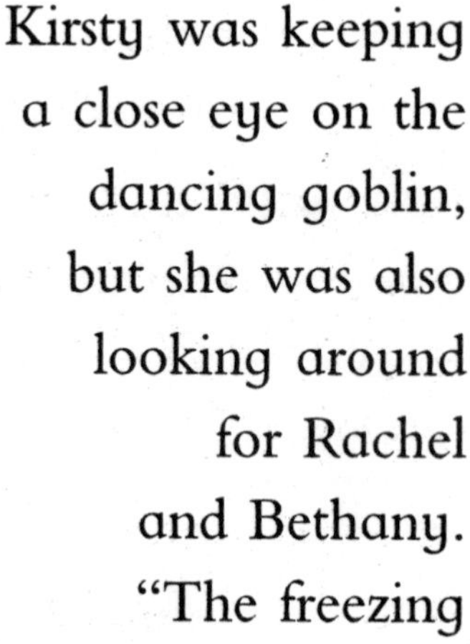

onto the stage below. Kirsty was keeping a close eye on the dancing goblin, but she was also looking around for Rachel and Bethany.

"The freezing spell's worn off and Kirsty's looking for us!" Rachel whispered to Bethany. "Maybe she can help us get the goblin underneath the moon."

Bethany nodded. "We'll have to be careful though," she whispered back. "We don't want the goblin to guess what we're up to!"

The little fairy waved her wand and a few magic sparkles drifted downwards, making Kirsty look up and spot her friends in the tree.

Rachel immediately pointed at the moon and then at the goblin, trying to explain to Kirsty that they needed him to be underneath the moon.

Rachel could see her friend frowning in concentration as she watched, but would she understand what Rachel wanted her to do?

Ballet Back on Track

For a moment Kirsty looked puzzled. Then she nodded and turned away. "I want that ribbon," she called to the goblin. "And don't even *think* of trying to freeze me again!"

The goblin scowled at her. "I can freeze you any time I want!" he snapped back.

"I don't think so!" Kirsty said mockingly.

Rachel and Bethany watched hopefully as Kirsty casually moved closer to the moon.

"I'll show you!" the goblin chuckled, skipping gleefully towards her.

Just a few more steps! Rachel thought, holding her breath. Kirsty moved away a little and the goblin followed, his hand outstretched to freeze her. Now he was right underneath the paper moon.

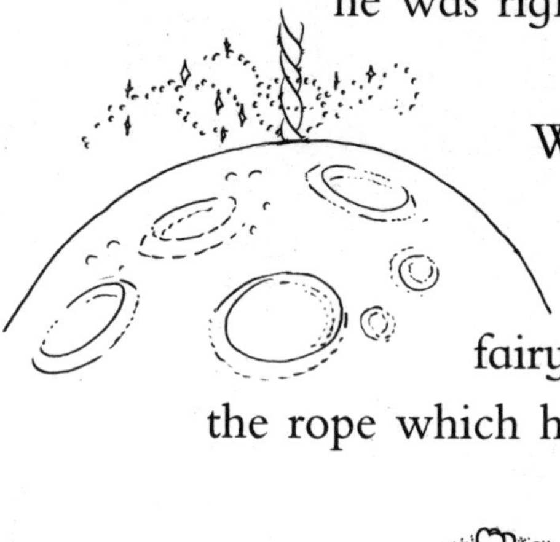

With a flick of her wrist Bethany sent a burst of fairy sparkles towards the rope which held the moon up.

The rope immediately untied itself and the moon plummeted, knocking the goblin to the floor.

"Agghh!" the goblin yelled in surprise.

Quick as a flash, Kirsty whipped the magic ribbon from the goblin's head. He sat up, looking furious but unhurt.

She tried to jump aside as the goblin grabbed at her wrist but she wasn't quick enough. Rachel's heart skipped a beat as the goblin shouted, "Freeze!" once more.

But, this time, nothing happened! Kirsty looked relieved and waved up at her friends. "I'm fine!" she called. Bethany and Rachel flew down to join her.

"It looks like Jack Frost only gave you the freezing power while you had the ribbon," Bethany told the goblin with a grin.

Looking extremely sulky, the goblin

stuck his tongue out at her. "Well, we still have the other magic ribbons!" he snapped. "And I'll make sure we hang onto them!" Scowling, he jumped up and ran off.

"Thank you so much, girls!" Bethany said joyfully. She sent a stream of magic fairy dust towards the ribbon in Kirsty's hand and it floated over to the little fairy, shrinking down to its usual Fairyland size as it did so. As the girls watched, the ribbon reattached itself to Bethany's wand in a cloud of pink sparkles, shining an even deeper pink colour as it did so.

"Now, hurry back to your seats while I put everything right here on stage," Bethany told Rachel and Kirsty. "Everyone will be unfreezing soon, and the performance will begin. Thankfully, now that I have my ribbon back, it should go perfectly!"

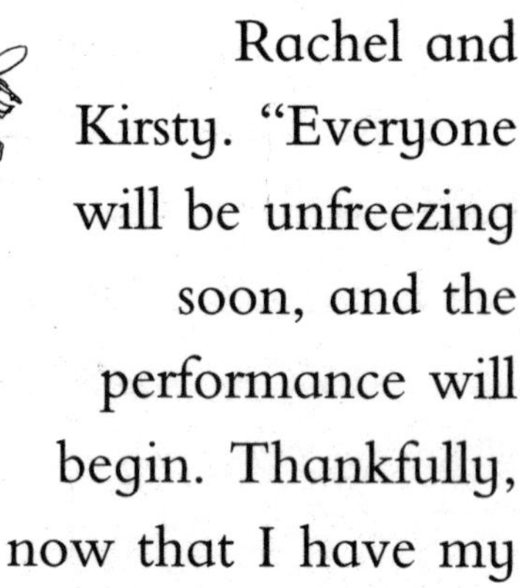

"Goodbye!" Rachel and Kirsty called to the fairy, hurrying towards the stage door. As they went, they saw the dancers and stagehands beginning to unfreeze.

"Let's get this show on the road!" one of the stagehands declared.

Rachel and Kirsty grinned at each other. Then they quickly bought a programme and dashed back to their seats.

"Just in time, girls!" whispered Mr Tate as they sat down. "The ballet's starting now."

Rachel and Kirsty gazed eagerly at the beautiful scene on the stage once more.

The paper moon was back in its proper place again, and seated on top of it was Bethany. Rachel and Kirsty smiled as the little fairy waved at them before vanishing in a puff of silvery-white sparkles.

"This is going to be great!" Rachel sighed happily as the dancers began to pirouette across the frozen lake on stage. "But we can't forget that we've got six more magic ribbons to find."

"Yes, and we'll have to be careful of the goblins' new freezing powers," Kirsty whispered. "Still, I can't wait for our next fairy adventure!"

The Dance Fairies

Bethany the Ballet Fairy has got her magic ribbon back. Now Rachel and Kirsty must help

Jade the Disco Fairy

BETHANY THE BALLET FAIRY 978-1-84616-490-3

JADE THE DISCO FAIRY 978-1-84616-491-0

REBECCA THE ROCK 'N' ROLL FAIRY 978-1-84616-492-7

TASHA THE TAP DANCE FAIRY 978-1-84616-493-4

JESSICA THE JAZZ FAIRY 978-1-84616-495-8

SASKIA THE SALSA FAIRY 978-1-84616-496-5

IMOGEN THE ICE DANCE FAIRY 978-1-84616-497-2

Win Rainbow Magic goodies!

In every book in the Rainbow Magic Dance Fairies series (books 50-56) there is a hidden picture of a ribbon with a secret letter in it. Find all seven letters and re-arrange them to make a special Dance Fairies word, then send it to us. Each month we will put the entries into a draw and select one winner to receive a Rainbow Magic Sparkly T-shirt and Goody Bag!

Send your entry on a postcard to Rainbow Magic Dance Fairies Competition, Orchard Books, 338 Euston Road, London NW1 3BH. Australian readers should write to Hachette Children's Books, Level 17/207 Kent Street, Sydney, NSW 2000. New Zealand readers should write to Rainbow Magic Competition, 4 Whetu Place, Mairangi Bay, Auckland, NZ. Don't forget to include your name and address. Only one entry per child. Final draw: 30th September 2008.

Good luck!

The Rainbow Fairies

Ruby the Red Fairy	ISBN	978 1 84362 016 7
Amber the Orange Fairy	ISBN	978 1 84362 017 4
Saffron the Yellow Fairy	ISBN	978 1 84362 018 1
Fern the Green Fairy	ISBN	978 1 84362 019 8
Sky the Blue Fairy	ISBN	978 1 84362 020 4
Izzy the Indigo Fairy	ISBN	978 1 84362 021 1
Heather the Violet Fairy	ISBN	978 1 84362 022 8

The Weather Fairies

Crystal the Snow Fairy	ISBN	978 1 84362 633 6
Abigail the Breeze Fairy	ISBN	978 1 84362 634 3
Pearl the Cloud Fairy	ISBN	978 1 84362 635 0
Goldie the Sunshine Fairy	ISBN	978 1 84362 636 7
Evie the Mist Fairy	ISBN	978 1 84362 637 4
Storm the Lightning Fairy	ISBN	978 1 84362 638 1
Hayley the Rain Fairy	ISBN	978 1 84362 641 1

The Party Fairies

Cherry the Cake Fairy	ISBN	978 1 84362 818 7
Melodie the Music Fairy	ISBN	978 1 84362 819 4
Grace the Glitter Fairy	ISBN	978 1 84362 820 0
Honey the Sweet Fairy	ISBN	978 1 84362 821 7
Polly the Party Fun Fairy	ISBN	978 184362 822 4
Phoebe the Fashion Fairy	ISBN	978 1 84362 823 1
Jasmine the Present Fairy	ISBN	978 1 84362 824 8

The Jewel Fairies

India the Moonstone Fairy	ISBN	978 1 84362 958 0
Scarlett the Garnet Fairy	ISBN	978 1 84362 954 2
Emily the Emerald Fairy	ISBN	978 1 84362 955 9
Chloe the Topaz Fairy	ISBN	978 1 84362 956 6
Amy the Amethyst Fairy	ISBN	978 1 84362 957 3
Sophie the Sapphire Fairy	ISBN	978 1 84362 953 5
Lucy the Diamond Fairy	ISBN	978 1 84362 959 7

The Pet Keeper Fairies

Katie the Kitten Fairy	ISBN	978 1 84616 166 7
Bella the Bunny Fairy	ISBN	978 1 84616 170 4
Georgia the Guinea Pig Fairy	ISBN	978 1 84616 168 1
Lauren the Puppy Fairy	ISBN	978 1 84616 169 8
Harriet the Hamster Fairy	ISBN	978 1 84616 167 4
Molly the Goldfish Fairy	ISBN	978 1 84616 172 8
Penny the Pony Fairy	ISBN	978 1 84616 171 1

The Fun Day Fairies

Megan the Monday Fairy	ISBN	978 184616 188 9
Tallulah the Tuesday Fairy	ISBN	978 1 84616 189 6
Willow the Wednesday Fairy	ISBN	978 1 84616 190 2
Thea the Thursday Fairy	ISBN	978 1 84616 191 9
Freya the Friday Fairy	ISBN	978 1 84616 192 6
Sienna the Saturday Fairy	ISBN	978 1 84616 193 3
Sarah the Sunday Fairy	ISBN	978 1 84616 194 0

The Petal Fairies

Tia the Tulip Fairy	ISBN	978 1 84616 457 6
Pippa the Poppy Fairy	ISBN	978 1 84616 458 3
Louise the Lily Fairy	ISBN	978 1 84616 459 0
Charlotte the Sunflower Fairy	ISBN	978 1 84616 460 6
Olivia the Orchid Fairy	ISBN	978 1 84616 461 3
Danielle the Daisy Fairy	ISBN	978 1 84616 462 0
Ella the Rose Fairy	ISBN	978 1 84616 464 4

The Dance Fairies

Bethany the Ballet Fairy	ISBN	978 1 84616 490 3
Jade the Disco Fairy	ISBN	978 1 84616 491 0
Rebecca the Rock'n'Roll Fairy	ISBN	978 1 84616 492 7
Tasha the Tap Dance Fairy	ISBN	978 1 84616 493 4
Jessica the Jazz Fairy	ISBN	978 1 84616 495 8
Saskia the Salsa Fairy	ISBN	978 1 84616 496 5
Imogen the Ice Dance Fairy	ISBN	978 1 84616 497 2

Holly the Christmas Fairy	ISBN	978 1 84362 661 9
Summer the Holiday Fairy	ISBN	978 1 84362 960 3
Stella the Star Fairy	ISBN	978 1 84362 869 9
Kylie the Carnival Fairy	ISBN	978 1 84616 175 9
Paige the Pantomime Fairy	ISBN	978 1 84616 209 1
Flora the Fancy Dress Fairy	ISBN	978 1 84616 505 4
The Rainbow Magic Treasury	ISBN	978 1 84616 047 9
Fairy Fashion Dress-Up Book	ISBN	978 1 84616 371 5
Fairy Friends Sticker Book	ISBN	978 1 84616 370 8
Fairy Stencils Sticker Colouring Book		978 1 84616 476 7
Fairy Style Fashion Sticker Book		978 1 84616 478 1

Coming soon:

Chrissie the Wish Fairy	ISBN	978 1 84616 506 1

All priced at £3.99.
Holly the Christmas Fairy, Summer the Holiday Fairy, Stella the Star Fairy, Kylie the Carnival Fairy, Paige the Pantomime Fairy, Flora the Fancy Dress Fairy and *Chrissie the Wish Fairy* are priced at £5.99. *The Rainbow Magic Treasury* is priced at £12.99.
Rainbow Magic books are available from all good bookshops, or can be ordered direct from the publisher: Orchard Books, PO BOX 29, Douglas IM99 1BQ
Credit card orders please telephone 01624 836000
or fax 01624 837033 or visit our Internet site: www.orchardbooks.co.uk
or e-mail: bookshop@enterprise.net for details.

To order please quote title, author and ISBN and your full name and address.
Cheques and postal orders should be made payable to 'Bookpost plc.'
Postage and packing is FREE within the UK
(overseas customers should add £2.00 per book).
Prices and availability are subject to change.